The Flower of Life

Nora Knight

PublishAmerica
Baltimore

First printing

ISBN: 1-60441-786-2
PUBLISHED BY PUBLISHAMERICA, LLLP
www.publishamerica.com
Baltimore

Printed in the United States of America

Acknowledgments:

I would like to thank everyone who volunteered their time and energy to help me with editorial revisions of this book, as it was a challenge for me to create a literary work in the language that was not my native language—your help is deeply appreciated; the staff at PublishAmerica for their support during the publishing of this book; all people who gave me encouragement and support during the most difficult times of my life—it will stay in my heart forever; everyone who inspired me with their act of kindness, compassion, and generosity to write this book in hopes that it would help other people to open their doors to hope and renewed faith.

Part I

1

It was late fall. Brown, crinkled-up leaves were scattered by chilly winds along both sides of the road. Naked tree branches froze in the cold air, outlining a gray sky. I felt cozy and secure in my family circle. Our big old house sheltered us from the wind and the cold. The day was no different from many other days we spent together as a family. Maybe that is why we took it for granted. The kids were trying to get ready for bedtime, using their creative excuses to get any chance not to go to sleep. Zachary and I were sitting and chatting at the small round kitchen table, while he finished his bottle of beer.

I was trying to convince him that it isn't safe to carry a gun without a license, and that he shouldn't be riding a motorcycle this time of year. I told him about the feeling I had had deep inside me for quite some time, a feeling of impending danger. I didn't know why I felt that way, but I felt it so strongly that I could no longer keep the restless feeling all to myself. He, as always, didn't take it seriously.

"Don't worry," he comforted me as usual, brushing it off: "I'm experienced. I've been driving for many years. Nothing can happen to me. And as for the gun, no one will find out that I carry it," he reassured me, hiding it in the inside left chest pocket of his black leather jacket. "I just carry it for protection," he added as if defending himself.

He smiled carelessly with a big smile of a little boy who just got a shiny new toy. Finally, after a long stressful day, the children were asleep, and he headed into the bedroom. I shut off all the lights and snuggled up with him under a puffy blanket, wrapping myself into his warm big palms. *What magic hands he has,* I thought. *They make me forget all my worries.* I felt the softness of his skin pressing against my back and the firmness of his strong young body. We fell asleep.

2

I didn't notice that Zachary snuck out of bed at night, heading to work on his motorcycle. While being lost in my dreams, I could hear the distant ringing of our phone. I opened my eyes for a moment to see what time it was. *Six o'clock in the morning. Why,* I thought to myself, trying to hold on to the vivid memories of my dream and to process the ringing of the phone at the same time, *why is someone trying to reach us this early?* But I brushed off those thoughts instantly. I decided that it couldn't be anything so serious that was worth for me getting out of bed to answer the call at this hour. *It's time to get up anyways,* I admitted to myself sadly. My job was waiting for me, and no excuses would bring peace when you know it's time to get up to go to work. I turned onto my right side, pulling the puffy blanket up to my chin, trying to memorize how cozy the warmth of my bed feels like. My eyes finally opened, and I took a deep breath. The window next to my bed was opened just enough for the fresh air to fill the room. The air felt cold and crisp, like it usually feels in the late fall.

I got myself out of bed, made a cup of coffee, and got my four-year-old daughter up getting her ready for daycare. I was ready for this little devil this time. I offered her two outfits to choose from, and she felt like she was the one making decision on what she will wear today. She calmly picked one of the two outfits I set aside for her. *Good job, Mom. That went smoothly,* I congratulated myself. *No fights this morning about what my little girl will agree to wear,* I told myself catching a smile on my own face.

My two-year-old son and the rest of my family were still asleep. Even though my son stayed with people who loved him as much as I do, it was hard leaving my baby home. I went into his room and sat down next to him, trying to capture the peaceful look on his precious face. His little hands were resting just above his head. I kissed his tiny fingers and forehead. *Somebody told me, when the baby sleeps with his hands above his head it means they are happy,* I remembered, and I ran my fingers through his soft hair. I left his room on my tiptoes and quietly closed the door to his room behind me.

I was ready to start my business day, filling my head with job-related thoughts that were put on hold yesterday. I remembered the early morning phone call. Having an extra couple of minutes on my hands, I decided to listen to the phone message quickly.

3

The voice on the phone said calmly:

"Hello, I'm calling you from the hospital emergency room. Everything is OK. I don't want you to worry, but your husband is going to have surgery."

The message machine beeped loudly, breaking the peaceful silence of the morning, leaving me in complete confusion and panic. Thoughts one by one started rushing through my head. *It can't be happening to my husband. Surgery? What kind of surgery? He didn't plan to have any. We don't even have health insurance. They must have confused the phone number with somebody else's. If he needs surgery then something must have happened to him. It must be a mistake. No. Or is it possible that he's hurt really bad? Oh, no. It can't be true. I need him. What if he dies? How could something happen to my husband, the person I love, the person who is my security. My island where I can escape to, someone who I can forget about all my worries with. A person who offered me comfort, support, and protection for 8 years? How could this happen to him when he's only 28 years old? It could not happen to someone who's as strong as he is, tall as he is, young as he is, someone who has wide shoulders as he does, big muscular arms, big warm palms.*

Panic took over my whole body. I nervously paced from one room to another trying to analyze what could've happened to him. Instead of dropping my daughter off to the daycare, I called there and explained that she was going to the hospital with me. I did not know why I was taking her with me, but I knew that I was about to face something I was not ready to face alone, and my daughter was the fragile connection between the life I was leaving and the new life that I was about to enter. We jumped in the car and headed straight to the hospital. I wished my car had wings. Leaving my yard, I had quickly noticed that the road was covered with a thick heavy fog.

I can't see at all, I thought again. *How will I ever get there if I can't see where I am going?* My heart raced to the hospital, while my mind was aware that I had to drive very slowly, as I could see nothing. *I have never seen a fog this thick before*, I thought again, starting to feel the strange feeling of impending *danger* I have carried with me all these days. The more I analyzed it, the more questions popped into my head, the more worried my heart became. The highway was no different than back roads. There was no visibility. It seemed as if I had been driving for hours. Finally, I reached my exit. I turned the wheel with my clenched fingers and stopped at the red light, waiting impatiently for it to turn green.

4

I drove up to the hospital, and I parked my car in front of the emergency room entrance. That was it. We were here. I was about to enter the hospital and find out just which turn my life would take. Holding hands together, my daughter and I ran into the emergency room. Catching my breath I asked for help. The nurse at the desk asked me to wait. *Wait!* my heart was screaming inside me, *I can't wait any longer!* She looked through the list with names of people admitted to the emergency room earlier and, looking suspiciously at me, she asked me with hesitation if I was sure Zachary was in this hospital. She looked through the list again and, shaking her head in helplessness, she passed the list to another nurse. No one was able to find my husband's name. He didn't seem to exist anymore. Fear embraced me from head to toe, and I got goose bumps all over my body. I was startled at the thought that he might already be dead, and that is why they can't find his name. Emergency room employees told me that he was no longer there and that I should go home.

With the remainder of what was left from hope, I started to beg them if I could have a quick peek at the list with my own eyes. On a white piece of paper there were names and names of people admitted there that day. *Only the name is left from a person when one dies,* I thought, swallowing the lump in my throat. Some manager came into the room. Noticing me looking through the paperwork, she scolded me that I'm not supposed to be looking at these lists. My heart sank. But just as she pulled the papers out of my clenched fingers, my eyes reached his name at that very moment. *Oh! what a miracle!* I thought. *He's here! He's at the hospital.*

"Our floor doesn't have him," the manager blurted out. And she suggested that I come up to the trauma intensive care unit.

TICU? That must have been a mistake. I had a handsome, young, strong, healthy husband, a father of two small children. It must have been a mistake, I thought.

"Where are we going, Mommy? What happened, Mommy?" my daughter kept asking me, interrupting my frightened mind.

"It is going to be ok," I kept repeating, not knowing whether I was trying to answer her, or if I was telling her this to calm myself.

5

Feeling weak and worried, holding tight my little girl's small hand, I headed to TICU. As we entered the elevator, and its big heavy body started moving up to the fifth floor of the hospital, filling the air with dull sounds. The door opened, and we walked out into TICU. I could feel right away that this floor was different. The white walls and floors reminded me of how sterile everything was kept here. As we were passing the waiting room, I noticed the other visitors waiting for their loved ones. Some wept with no trace of hope left in their hearts. Their bodies were shaking, and their faces showed that they were in great pain. Others were comforting them with warm hugs or by compassionately holding their hands. Some were sitting quietly, staring at the empty yellow walls, as if awaiting for their verdict to be announced by the doctor. The place reminded me of the train station, except the trains were going in two directions only: life and death. Everybody was waiting for their train. With pain striking panic I started to wonder: *What train will we catch today?*

A nurse came up to me, as if she knew I was coming. Without any questions she explained to me that she'll invite the social worker for me. *Why would I need a social worker?* I was wondering to myself. *Do I need to fill out any forms for the surgery?* All I could find out from the nurses was that Zachary had been on his motorcycle this morning heading to work when he crashed. He was still in the operating room. They told me I had several hours in front of me just to wait for the surgery to end. They wouldn't tell me what was wrong with Zachary. *What kind of surgery did he agree to?* I wondered, not realizing just how hurt he must've been if the surgery took that long.

They asked me not to leave the waiting room. I sat down on the chair and looked around me. The person next to me wept quietly, wiping her tears with a tissue. I asked her what happened. A shriek of sorrow burst out of her mouth. She wept harder, as if I caused her more pain by asking the question. She kept repeating the same words in a language that I couldn't understand. I bent down and gave her a hug. The woman started crying even louder. In broken English, she asked me:

"Why? Why? Why my son? He was only 19! Why did God take him away from me?!"

The words of comfort that I was about to say got stuck in my throat. I put my arms around her. But nothing could bring her comfort. Another person came up to talk to her. I got up and started pacing impatiently from wall to wall, like a caged lion. Time was not moving. It felt as if I'd spent a few horrible, long days in this hospital. I tried to concentrate on our day-to-day life. The life we lived before the accident. I made some calls to his and my work, to our family, to let them know that our life is taking a change. No one was ready for this news, especially where I didn't have much information on his condition. When I called his work without explanation as to what exactly happened, his manager got very angry.

"He better return the truck keys!" she yelled with irritation in her voice. "He has a job to do today," she added. "I have no one to do it for him."

I had nothing to say to her, wondering if he'd be fired. I called home. My family didn't know what to say either. And I couldn't say when I'd be back, or when he'd be back. My confusion about the situation grew stronger. It was difficult to wait all these hours, not really knowing what's happened. It was very apparent that our life would not be the same any more. How much it will change? I did not know. Waiting was all I could do at the moment.

6

As I was waiting for my husband to magically appear healthy after his surgery and explain to me what all this meant, I saw a big group of nurses that surrounded a patient. They were running while pushing the stretcher, passing me. *This guy is in pretty bad shape,* I thought to myself, because they were running with tools around him, trying to get oxygen into him through a big tube that was sticking out of his blue mouth. It looked as if they were trying to save his life. *Poor man*, I thought to myself, watching the stretcher getting closer and closer to me. As they passed me, I saw the patient's white lifeless body, his droopy hands were hanging down from stretcher and bouncing in all directions. His face was the face of a dead person; his lips were blue. It was then that I recognized my husband's face in him. My mouth opened involuntarily, and his name slipped off my lips, leaving my body breathless.

I felt as if a massive bolt of lightning struck me. I felt paralyzed. I was standing and couldn't feel my feet, or the floor, or see people around me. The world froze in silence, or maybe, I had lost my hearing for a few minutes. My heart stopped. My life crushed before my eyes. I was left there standing and sensing how close the death was, and the emptiness of my life without my loved one being there for me. It felt as if I was standing on the edge of a tall cliff, sensing the wind in the open hollow in front of me, and the life I lived that was still behind my back. All my life I was in control of everything. And now, I felt powerless and helpless in front of a circumstance I could not control. His pale body lay there with no sign of life in it. His eyes were closed, his face was swollen probably twice its usual size. He had a big tube in his mouth. The nurses, noticing my reaction tried to hide him from me covering him with their hands and backs.

"But it is me!" I yelled feeling even more confused. "It is me, his wife!"

I was not allowed to come closer to him or even enter his room yet. His stretcher disappeared at the end of the long corridor. My body collapsed into the chair near me and, shaking like a leaf in the wind, I wept.

7

People that were waiting behind me silently came up to me and embraced me in their arms, while wiping my tears off my scared face. Someone showed me into a small conference room. My curious daughter started to get herself familiar with the contents of the room. She kept babbling some silly words. Her tiny voice still connected me to this life, the life I had to go on with regardless of what I have just witnessed. The door to our room opened, and the social worker came in. She was a woman in her fifties, very elegantly dressed, with white and gray hair. She sympathetically handed tissues to me and started asking me questions, disrupting my worries. I couldn't concentrate on her questions, as my mind was with Zachary, but she knew what to do and how to help me. She asked me if I wanted to take his clothes, or what was left of his clothes, home. I agreed. Then she brought me a big black bag. I opened it and started to take out his belongings one by one.

His red helmet was not even scratched. His black leather jacket had only one rip, in the place where he carried his gun. The gun was no longer there, nor was it in the bag with the rest of his stuff. *What happened to the gun?* I silently wondered. His torn clothes were radiating the familiar sweet smell of his body, and were ripped badly with the knives of the paramedics. There was his cross he never used to take off his neck, his wedding band he never used to take off his finger. I was actually doing it. I was going through his things, without even knowing if he would ever wear them again. I was breathing in the smell of his body for maybe the last time in my life. My husband's white lifeless body was in front of my eyes. With my shaking hands that stopped listening to me, I put his cross and the wedding ring through the broken chain and tied it around my neck, as if it could keep me closer to him. Rolling tears came down my pale cheeks. My daughter was constantly interrupting my conversation with the social worker and, seeing me cry, she couldn't help it but reassured me:

"Mommy, he's not broken in half, he's just hurt a little. He'll be OK. Please don't cry."

She was my connection, my fragile bridge between the death I touched and the life I was still living. The social worker asked me if I'm ready to talk to the doctor who operated on him. I couldn't wait for this moment, hoping that the doctor would bring me some reassuring, hopeful news. The door opened, and the doctor walked in. He had dark hair and dark eyes, and looked young and confident. With calm expression on his face, he looked at me studying my eyes. Then he quickly explained to me what Zachary lost, and what was fixed in his body. He couldn't tell if my husband would live or die, or if he'd become crippled as a result of accident. He said:

"I am just a doctor. I can only do what I can. I don't control the process of dying and living. There is someone who is more powerful who controls that. Your husband is in critical condition. He damaged a kidney, lost his spleen, ripped his intestines, his arm, leg, and a couple of vertebras were broken. We stopped the internal bleeding. We did everything we could."

As he had nothing else to tell me, and I could not think of any questions, the doctor stood up and left the room. The social worker explained that when the accident happened, Zachary was on his way to work on his motorcycle. It was a very foggy morning, and the glass of his helmet got covered with drops of water. He could see nothing, so while he tried to lift the glass of his helmet, his glasses got covered with water too. It took a few seconds for him to go off the road and crash. She explained that luckily, some woman was following him in her car, as she was going to work. She saw him fall, and she was the one who called 911. The social worker explained that if it was not for this woman, he would not be alive, because he was bleeding internally. The door opened again, and someone walked into our room. I was invited to see my husband. The social worker offered to stay with my little girl.

8

I walked down the long corridor and entered his room. Everything in it seemed to be white: the walls, his sheets, the color of his skin. He was there with a big tube in his blue mouth, his swollen face had no trace of life in it. The machine was breathing for him, making loud suction sounds. One of his arms was wrapped in a thick long cast. His big hands were resting along his body, that I just had in my arms last night, before the accident happened. I touched his hand but it didn't move. There was no sign of life in his big, what used to be strong, body. My love, everything I lived for, was between life and death. And my heart felt like it was ready to burst from sorrow. I felt so weak that for a moment I thought I was going to collapse on the floor, and I took a few steps toward the wall, to give my body some support. As I headed for the exit, I caught someone's glance at the corner of his room, a glance filled with compassion and understanding. It was real. It was happening to ME. I was not dreaming. I was left there to live, to take care of myself, my two small children, and with little hope, to take care of my dear love too, who was so helpless at that moment. Someone brought a chair for me. I sat down, buried my hands under his big cold palms, and let my tears come. He lay there so helpless. His eyes were shut, and I could feel that it was just his corpse lying on this bed. He did not seem to be inside it. I slowly got up and headed out of his room.

The social worker helped me to sort out my feelings and thoughts. It was apparent that my life was taking another direction. I was in charge of my family. I, who was deeply wounded, was in charge of making all decisions for myself, my hurt husband, and my two little kids. Questions rushed through my head. *Will I make it financially? How will we live? How can I work, take care of my husband, take care of kids, and do it all at the same time?* I was scared. I was horrified. I felt lost. The social worker made all the necessary calls to both of our jobs, explaining what happened and that my husband was in critical condition. It seemed like his manager would take care of disability insurance for him. It appeared things were going to be temporarily taken care of, but my mind wouldn't want to stop worrying about them. It could find no peace, no place to rest, no comfort.

9

I went back home to drop off my little girl. I gathered my family and explained that I would need their help with the kids. I knew I could not do it alone. For some reason, the first thing I wanted to do was to take a bath. I wanted to feel clean, wanted to wash away the sorrow and pain I felt so strongly. I was getting ready to fight for Zachary's life with something mysterious, something that I couldn't even see. I could feel this powerful spirit of danger floating around me, floating around him. I was preparing myself to help him fight death. I packed all the things I needed, including a pillow, so that I could sleep in the waiting room at the hospital if needed. I decided I would not leave him until I saw a sign of life in him again. I kissed my kids good bye and was on my way to the hospital.

When I was a couple of blocks away from my home, I realized that his cross and his wedding ring were no longer on me. The chain that I tied around my neck at the hospital must have been broken or untied. It startled me. I pulled over to the nearest parking lot and stopped the car. *Is it a sign? Does it mean that he will die? Does it mean God will not protect him? Does it mean I will lose the person I love?* I kept panicking. Suddenly, something calm and graceful entered my heart. *He will be fine,* I felt. *It was just a piece of metal that I lost at home.* I felt that God's love was there with me, it was right in my heart. I could feel its warmth inside of me. I turned my car around and headed to the hospital.

10

As I reached TICU, the nurses rushed to me to inform me that there was the police officer who was hoping to talk to my husband and me. They said that Zachary had a gun on him at the time of the accident, and the police officer seemed very concerned that he carried a gun without a license. Because there was a weapon involved, they were wondering if his accident was something more than just him falling off the motorcycle due to fog. The feeling of danger took over my mind immediately. I was anticipating it would come to this, but I was not sure what would the consequences be. Swallowing the lump in my throat, I concentrated on my mission. I was ready to do whatever it takes to help my love.

That day, to my biggest disappointment, I had learned that I couldn't stay with him all the time. The chair in the waiting room was the only place for me to get some sleep. When nurses were done working on him, they called me into his room. I walked in slowly and looked around the room. In the opposite corner there was another patient. As I found out later, she was a mother of four kids. She was also recovering from a car accident and was in critical condition. She lost her arm and shoulder, and had a brain injury. She had spent a week here already. Her husband was there in the waiting room, crying and sharing his feelings with others about how intelligent she was before the accident happened, and how doctors said she may never recover from her brain damage. He told us that at the time of the car accident she was in her car with her children. But it was only her who almost got killed. She was sitting on the bed and rocking herself back and forth, repeating the same words monotonously, as if she was emotionally detached from her wrecked body:

"It hurts, it hurts everywhere."

Nurses came in to work on her, and they closed the curtain around her. I looked at Zachary's pale lifeless body. A lump came up to my throat again. His monitor showed that he was in a lot of pain. I pulled up a chair and sat down next to him. I comforted my little hand under his big lifeless palm and opened the bible with another hand. I started praying to God for a miracle. Once in a while I would stand up and look in his face, hoping to find some sign of life in it. I'd whisper in his ears:

"You, I, and God are very powerful together. I need you! You can not leave me here alone. I love you, and I want you to fight for your life."

11

A few days had passed. Seeing no changes in him, I pleaded with the doctor to tell me that he will survive. But the answer remained the same. Zachary was still in critical condition. Very shortly a visitor knocked on the door of his room. The door opened, and his manager walked into his room. She introduced herself to me and glanced at his lifeless body, at what was left of him. She stood there for a few minutes, speechless. Then she turned to me, looked into my eyes, and squeezed the words "take care of yourself" leaving the room.

As I sat there, the more I accepted the reality, the more my mind was consumed with thoughts about his gun. I couldn't stop worrying about it. I went back home to talk to my relatives, hoping to find some comfort and to relieve the anxiety I could no longer take. They were religious people, and I was sure they could give me the comfort I needed.

"Do you know that he crashed on the motorcycle because of you?" they asked me in their cold curt voice. "You are paying for your sins, you cursed your husband," they added. "We will pray for you now, and we want you to pray with us, and to ask God to forgive your sins!" they ordered to me coldly.

I tried to hold myself together as best I could, so I just kept quiet while they said their prayer. It did not feel like God, but perhaps I was a big sinner that they were right about this. I knew that their son had the magazine, the one Zachary ordered the gun from. All I wanted was to get that magazine, so I could show the police what type of gun it was. I wanted them to clarify the consequences. It was better to know what we were facing, than to feel left hanging with no understanding of what is going to happen. I needed to know that he would not go to prison for it if he gets better. I needed it to finally let go of worries that were paralyzing me.

Their son promised to come for his lunch break and to look for the information I needed. As they finished their prayer, the door swung open and their son walked into the room. The first thing he did when he got into the apartment was walk straight to me and put his big arms around me, saying nothing at all. Suddenly, I could no longer control my emotions. A loud cry, like a cry of a badly hurt animal, escaped from my chest. I wept in his arms until I had no more tears to shed. He had nothing to say, but he was there with me in this most difficult moment. Once I calmed down, he found the magazine for me.

12

The next day on my way to the hospital, I decided to stop by the police station. I wanted to ask a few questions about the gun. I was hoping to relieve my anxiety related to it. At the police station, some police officers in blue, creased uniforms were socializing. They had big smiles on their relaxed faces. I hesitantly came up to the window.

"May I help you?" said the officer, noticing me standing in hesitation.

I showed him the magazine and asked what would happen if my husband had a gun on him without the license. Shaken up by the September 11 terrorist attacks, police officers asked me sternly to come into the office to talk. I sat down in the office, my heart could not stop racing. *Did it mean I came to collect bad news? All I wanted was the answer for a small question. It definitely did not mean anything good,* I thought to myself. The officer walked into the room, and started to fill out the paperwork on me. He asked for my name, address, citizenship, and collected all of the information about Zachary. He was looking at me very suspiciously, carefully watching the expression of my face. When I said that I do not want to answer any questions, nor do I have time for this, because I have a husband in the TICU in critical condition, the officer became furious. He stated that I can't leave his office, until I give him all the information he needs. Tears came rushing down my face. As much as I wanted to control my shaking body, I had no luck in doing so. The officer started to doubt that I was in suitable condition for driving my car. He asked me if I was seeing a psychiatrist on a regular basis. He asked if I had kids, and when I said that they are at the daycare, he called there to make sure that my kids were in a safe place.

It was obvious that I was not going to get let go, until I give them all the information about me and Zachary, so I gave it all to them, feeling like I was stripped of my personality, like I was raped emotionally. The officer called the hospital. He confirmed that my husband was in critical condition. As the end result of this deposition, I finally found out, that if he did not retrieve the gun from the police office, he would not be charged with anything. The emotional rape was over. I was told that the police officers would not let me drive my car to the hospital, as they feel I should not be driving in this condition. I had no one to call for a ride to the hospital, and my heart was racing from the thought that I spent so many hours here, while I felt I should be next to the person, who were hanging there by a thread, alone and very hurt.

I was left alone, sitting in that office. The emotional pain was excruciating. The door opened once again, and a different police officer came into the room. He looked at me with compassion and explained to me that he got a permission from his manager to give me a ride to the hospital. Tears poured down my cheeks. He extended his warm hand to me, and I hesitantly grabbed it, thankful that someone cared to help. He walked me out to the police car and opened the door of the car for me. I climbed into the back seat, feeling wet and cold from tears and sweat. I hugged myself, putting my arms around me, trying to calm my body from shaking.

13

While I was on my way to the hospital, the police officer called there, asking the social worker to meet me in the lobby. The same, friendly and compassionate social worker was waiting for me when I arrived at the hospital.

"What happened?" she asked me in disbelief.

I sat down next to her in the lobby and told her the story, scaring away hospital visitors with my hysterical crying. I then told her how my relatives think it was all a punishment for my sins. I described how Zachary was the nicest person, how I always felt that I did not deserve to be with such a nice person, and now I was here and healthy, while he was so hurt and suffering. She took my hand, and comforting me with kind words, she walked me to the elevator.

While nurses were working on Zachary, I went down and sat on the bench outside the hospital. I clenched my fingers, looked up at the sky, and wept quietly, swallowing lumps in my throat. The words of my relatives, that I cursed my husband and now I am paying for my sins, were ringing in my ears. The horror I felt at the police station felt like a fresh wound in my heart. I raised my eyes to the sky and yelled out:

"I don't believe God exists!" I kept looking at the gray sky, as if hoping to receive an answer from it. A woman visitor came up to my bench and sat next to me. She sat there quietly, probably thinking of her own tragedy. Then she asked me why I was here. I told her about what happened, and she assured me that God knows everything and He will come to help. As we sat outside on that bench, I noticed a stranger who was walking towards the hospital with roses in her hands. She seemed to be moving in our direction from the street. To my complete surprise, she came up to me, opened my clenched fingers, and put two petals of a rose in the palm of my hand. She looked right at me. Her beautiful blue eyes radiated kindness, and her face was lit up with a compassionate smile.

"God sent me to you to give you the flower of life," she said to me in a confident, pleasant voice.

For a few moments I froze speechless, looking in her big blue eyes, finding all the caring humanity in them that I so desperately needed. Her glance said that she brought the strength I needed to go on, and that I should not hesitate any more that help is on the way. She lit up the hope in my torn-up heart. The woman visitor, who was sitting next to me, whispered that she got chills up her spine. The stranger with the rose turned around, and walked away from the hospital.

I got up and ran up to the elevators. Reaching the TICU, I flew out of the elevator and ran straight to his room. I bent down to him, and whispered that God had sent him life, that we would make it through our rough times. I had hidden the rose petals in the cast on his arm, hoping that they would remain near his body until he is safe. I prayed to God that He would breathe my love and my life into Zachary's body. I prayed that he would take everything beautiful and pure from inside my heart, and transfer it into him. As I whispered in his ears that I wouldn't survive without him and that I wanted him to fight for his life, I noticed a tear rolling down his cheek. He could hear me! I reached him! He was there! I squeezed his big hand and kissed it.

14

The hospital crew collected some money for us, and as I entered home my parents started to tell me excitedly how there were people here at our house. They came from the hospital and they brought us groceries. They told me that there were also people from Zachary's work who brought us boxes with food and the money they collected for us. As I was listening to the blessings my parents were sharing with me, our neighbors knocked on the door. They brought us some money too. My manager called me, and said that they want me to be next to my husband, and that they will pay me for this time at a regular rate. Then, a manager from his work called. She also offered her help, and asked if there was anything she can do for us. We were not alone.

The doctor called me and explained about his condition. He said that they were planning to take the breathing tube out in a couple of days. And so they did. On that day, I was in the hospital, waiting outside of his room. It felt like a new life was going to be born. It felt like years passed since the last moment I spoke with my husband. I paced from wall to wall in the corridor, biting my nails impatiently. The door to his room swung wide open. It seemed like the light in his white room became even brighter. I saw Zachary in this bright light, sitting down on his stretcher. He was breathing on his own! He was looking at me! I ran into the room and looked into his eyes with a hunger to reconnect with him, trying to read the information off of them about what he might have felt at the moment. He looked at me, and moving his dry lips, he tried to tell me something. But he had no voice. The feeling that he was sitting and seeing me was thrilling.

The nurse opened his robe in front of me, and I saw a huge opening on his body from his heart to the bottom of his belly that was about four inches wide. He could not see it, because he still had a collar on his neck, in case his neck was damaged. He was cut like a pig, ready to be served for dinner. Big, wide, red elastics and staples held the meat of his front body together. The wound was bleeding. The picture was so terrifying that I had to turn away. My heart felt as if it was cut open. I turned back to him, and looked in his face. He looked like he was in agony but was not able to sound out the words to say it. *What did you do to yourself?* sat on the tip of my tongue. But instead, I shook my head and took his warm hand covering it with my small palms. I spent some more time with him, and feeling that he was on his way to getting better, I started to calm down. It was getting very late, and I asked him if it was ok for me to leave. He squeezed my hand as a symbol of acceptance. Oh, what a pleasure it was to feel that squeeze! I headed home, happy for the first time after the accident.

15

The darkness of the night was filled with a thick fog. It was hard to see where I was going, just like on the day of the accident. It gave me a feeling of hesitation whether the worst was over. It was three days since I had seen my children. As I walked into the house, my kids ran to me crying happily:

"Mom is here! Mom is here!"

They were dancing around me with big smiles on their faces. They were kissing me on my face, kissing my hands, hugging me tightly with their small arms. My daughter asked me if she could stay with me for the night. And I did not mind. I put my arms around her small body, feeling her warmth.

The phone rang; my friend was wondering how I was doing. Crying, I started to share with her all the pain that collected inside of me. While I was talking to her, my daughter was rubbing my back and was saying repeatedly in quiet voice:

"I love you, Mommy. I love you, Mommy."

I have never heard her saying these words before and never had her rubbing my back. I could not have thought a child that small could understand just how much pain I felt. It was a blessing to feel her little hands on my back and to hear her voice filled with caring and understanding.

We fell asleep together. The morning came and I went back to the hospital. To my complete horror, I found the machine was breathing for him again. His condition was critical again. Doctors explained to me that he vomited while he was getting a cat scan. And since he had a collar around his neck, he could not turn his head. The liquid he had to drink for the cat scan then entered his lungs. They said his condition now was even more critical than before. If he catches pneumonia, he might not make it without his spleen. Within the next couple of days we would find out if he would live . He had a very high fever, the expression of his face had the feel of suffering. He was shivering on his stretcher in his white room. I blamed myself for leaving him that night. *What did I do! Now I might lose him.* I couldn't forgive myself for leaving him when I had just got him back. They scheduled the procedure for his lungs. It was very painful, but he had to go through it. The nurses asked me to leave the room. I did, and they started to work on him right away. I could hear him gagging, while they were working on cleaning his lungs, and I could feel the pain, as if it was me who was going through the procedure. I clenched my fingers into fists, and begged God for help. All I could do was to wait.

The door opened, and they invited me back to the room again. I was told that they washed out his lungs the best they could. The rates on his monitor did not say anything good, his fever went up. I pulled up a chair next to him once again, grabbed his big hot hand, and opened the bible. The nurse walked into the room to check his fluids. She saw me reading the bible and started asking me questions about our situation. I told her that his mother is going to come over from a different country in a few days. I explained how hard it will be for me to work, bring her back and forth to the hospital every day, and take care of our kids, all at the same time. She looked at my bible and smiled at me with a kind big smile.

"God will take care of this," she said.

16

A few days went by, I was standing next to his bed. I had noticed that his behavior was rather strange. While he was heavily sedated, he made jerky movements with his hands and feet that he has not been doing before. I called the nurse, and not long afterward the doctors rushed into the room to check him out. Sure enough, they found that he had a rip in his intestines again, and they asked me to sign a paper allowing them to do another surgery on him. They said that they will try to fix his broken leg and arm at the same time, as it was not healing properly. I felt like I was signing his life away. He was taken to the OR again. Feeling empty and hopeless, I went to pick up his mother from the airport. She just came over from Russia, all worried and upset about her son's condition. It was hard for her to take the time off to come, but she managed to do it. Her co-workers collected the money for her plane ticket, after they found out that her son was in critical condition. After a long exhausting day in the air, she finally was here, a few hours away from seeing her dying son.

I briefly explained to her what had happened, telling about the never-ending battle for his life. I could feel how she was struggling, trying to breathe, as if trying to catch her breath every other minute. I knew it was even more difficult for her than it was for me, as I already accepted the situation. But it was still new to her, like a fresh wound. We drove at night, feeling tired, but anxious, passing the street lights. I parked my car near the hospital and we walked in. I could only imagine that she probably felt the same way I did, when entering the hospital, not knowing what I would face.

By the time we arrived in his room, he was back from his surgery. He was awake and his body was all shaking. His face begged for mercy, his eyes were filled with tears of fear. His lips were quivering, and a quiet crying was coming out of his mouth. His heart rate went up, and the nurse explained that she had a hard time stabilizing it. It was not only painful for him to go through it, but it was very painful to watch him in such agony, knowing that we could do nothing to relieve his pain. He knew we were in the room. He couldn't talk or turn his head to us. But his eyes were following us, begging for help. His mother was repeating with shaking voice:

"I am here my son, I am here with you."

Tears were rolling down his cheeks. Oh, what torture it must have been for him. The nurse ordered us out of his room. Speechless, we left obediently, trusting his life to her.

17

We were standing in the white corridor with our arms around each other. His mother was crying quietly on my shoulder. The head nurse peeked at us from a room at the end of the corridor and invited me into the conference room. She explained that his mother was given a free room to stay in, right here at the hospital, for as long as she needed it. She gave me the key to the room and put a thick pack of food coupons for the hospital cafeteria into my hands. She put her arms around me and wished me good luck. My heart felt so big; it was overwhelmed with gratitude for something I did not even expect. It was one more blessing that God sent to us though people we did not even know—a room we could not afford otherwise. A room that was so appreciated, while the person we loved needed comfort and care we would not have been able to give him otherwise.

Days went by, weeks, then months went by. There were days when we thought Zachary was getting better. There were also days when we thought we were about to lose him again, when his weakened body was taking us by surprise with new complications. Little by little, day by day he was nursed back to life. One day he sat up on his bed ready to be discharged. That day, I noticed that there was something under his bed. It was a dark color and did not fit in with the cleanliness of his white hospital room. I bent down, and to my complete surprise, I picked up the rose petals from under his bed. That was the flower that God sent to me by a stranger from the street, to give me hope. I was holding them in my hand, feeling the chills going up my spine. I opened the bible and hid the dried petals between the pages. The presence of God in my heart was stronger than ever. Feeling the grace of faith inside me I sent a letter to one of my depressed friends to cheer her up. In that letter, I wrote to her that God will send us different people, and that He will also take them away from us. That only God will be with us forever no matter what. He will always be there for us with his endless miracles.

The worst was over. We took him home, finally he was home. He still had four wide red elastics that were holding together his cut-up belly. While taking him for a walk in his wheelchair, I was breathing in the fresh air and looking at the beauty of the green forest. I noted how beautiful everything looked when the person you love is well and next to you. I thought of how lucky I was to have him alive. I knew that we would make it through the difficult times. I knew he would eventually get better. I believed that he would find the strength to go on, to enjoy life again once his overall condition would improve.

It was terrifying to look at his wound in the beginning, but eventually I learned how to change the dressing on it without fainting. Months passed, as I was nursing him back to life. Another year passed before he got himself out of the wheelchair and crutches. He was struggling to find a well-paying job. The right time came, and he finally got a job as a coach bus driver. Wearing a white shirt and black pants, handsome, full of energy and charm, he came back to the hospital to express his gratitude to the hospital crew that spent months on keeping him alive. He returned home, sharing with me how they did not even recognize him because he looked so healthy and happy, so full of life and energy, so different from the weak, hopeless guy who looked like a shadow of death when he left the hospital in his wheelchair.

18

Zachary did not remember much about what happened to him at the hospital. The only memories he had left were from when he got better and was on his way to a long but successful recovery. It was me who had all the memories of his critical condition, memories of his battle for life, memories of his sufferings and our helplessness burnt into my brain. My heart healed as the years went by, but it never was the same heart. He recovered from his trauma almost completely, and it seemed that this trauma did not change him. But I found that I was not the same anymore. Realizing how fragile human life was, I found it difficult to enjoy material things that used to bring me pleasure before the accident happened. I never stopped appreciating that I still had a husband, a person I deeply loved, and that my children had a father.

Part II

1

Five years went by. Years filled with love and support, caring and dedication to our family and to each other. Years of mutual respect and dreams about growing old together. Zachary and I went through many disappointments side by side, helping each other to get through rough times. We shared countless happy moments together. Everything seemed normal. And yet, the restless feeling has returned to me. I started to have vivid dreams that my husband left me for another woman and treated me very cruelly—as if we were never related to each other, as if I meant nothing to him. Each morning, I would wake up in a sweat. Every time I told him about these dreams, he would brush them off:

"Of course, I'm always the bad guy!"

Then he would reassure me that no one wants him because he has a long, ugly scar across his body. The scar was formed from uneven healing of muscle layers and body meat, as the healing progressed from inside his body and out to the skin. The scar was wide, bumpy, and brown—different from the rest of the skin on his white belly. He was very embarrassed by it and always covered it with a t-shirt when he went swimming. But I knew that I loved him regardless of his appearance. On an unconscious level, I felt that my love was not enough for him, but I couldn't find a logical explanation as to why I felt this way.

2

Our kids were growing up. Our son turned six and our daughter was nine. People commented that we were a model couple, an ideal family. Some were openly jealous of how we treated each other with utmost respect and that we were very good friends to each other. I simply enjoyed the comfort of him being next to me, the thought of him being alive, the thought that my children had their dad. I was glad that God gave him another chance at life and gave me another chance to feel his young body next to mine, to hear his voice, to have his support and comfort, to have him as my soul mate. It felt as a blessing to have another chance to enjoy our family, a chance to be cared for by a man who I felt was an inseparable part of me, a chance to care for him and to love.

I felt that his long-distance trips that lasted days, and sometimes weeks, robbed us of our precious time together. Explaining to me that his management was very strict, he said that he could not take any more weekends off. I was feeling very lonely, abandoned. It had been many years that I had been feeling that way. I devoted myself to my family completely, leaving my ambitions and goals behind. It felt as if I were a single mom, trying to deal with the difficulties of raising children and taking care of the house alone. It did not seem fair to me, but I accepted the situation as a part of adult life, to the point that I did not notice how I lost myself. He had been devoting himself to his job more and more. He loved his job, loved the opportunity to see new places and to meet new people. When I complained about feeling lonely and asked him to do something about the job, his answer was that he did not want to change. Job satisfaction meant more for him than our time together or his time together with the kids. In fact, it seemed that our children were irritating him, and he used any excuse to get away from us, even if it meant going shopping or fixing the car. He assured me that there was no other way to make the same income, and I trusted him. It hurt me that I had no help with the chores at home, no help with our children. That all the responsibilities were on my shoulders. It was painful that I couldn't get a job that would bring me the same satisfaction he so easily derived from his job. The kids needed at least one parent and I had to do what felt right, which was accepting the job that allowed me to be their mother. Someone had to take care of them, to be there for them when they were sick, to bring them to classes, teach them to read, bring them to socialize with their friends, and give them a supportive environment for learning and growing smarter. I was a mom, a doctor, a cook, a plumber, an entertainer, a maid, a teacher, a therapist. I was the whole world for them.

3

Even though Zachary was working a lot, and was hardly at home, it seemed we could not catch up with our bills. The income from the apartment upstairs stopped a year ago when our tenants moved out in the beginning of the spring. It was strange—we both worked, but financial burdens were choking us. I couldn't understand why we needed so much money to make ends meet. Spring was the time of year he made the most money. He was working every weekend, and yet we didn't have enough money in our joint account. It looked like he made many large withdrawals, but he said that he needed money to eat, because he spent most of his time away from home.

Panicking about our financial situation, I was intensively looking for new tenants. However, being very picky, he never agreed with any of the prospective tenants I found. One day, when he had just come from work, I told him that a woman called me about our ad in the newspaper. She was supposed to come over right when he walked in the door. When I told him her name, he seemed to be pleasantly surprised and said that she was his co-worker. A minute later, the phone rang, and she told me that some other plans had come up and she would not be able to make it. It felt strange that plans could have come up during the fifteen-minute period of time between her two phone calls. That day my husband had walked home from work instead of taking his car. The only logical explanation I could think of was that she saw him walking into our yard and realized that the house belonged to him. Perhaps she didn't want to rent from a co-worker, as it would take away from her privacy. He told me that he hesitated over whether he should ask her why she changed her mind about the apartment, but a week went by, and he told me that she would be renting from us.

She was in her late thirties, five years older than we were. She had worked with him for over two years as a bus driver. He said she had three children, 13, 16, and 18, and had custody of only one of them. He talked about her with admiration and utmost respect, convincing me that she and I would become best friends. Once she started renting from us, he stopped inviting his best friend over, who also worked with him at the same company. His friend was aware that we were looking for a tenant, and when I told him the story about her inquiring about our apartment, he warned me that this woman was nothing but trouble. I felt uneasy letting her in, but Zachary convinced me that she was the nicest person, and that he was confident that she would pay her rent on time, which would save our financial situation.

4

She had moved in alone. As she was here, I began to notice that there was some connection between my husband and her, something more than just a relationship between two co-workers. Each time he saw her, he was smiling with a smile I have not seen on his face for a long time. One day, when I shared with him my intuitive feelings about their relationship, he admitted to me that she was his best and only friend. Obviously, she was a friend he never told me about. But he never talked about his friends. He seemed to be annoyed by my worries about it, assuring me that there is nothing intimate between them. He asked me with suspicion if I had told anyone at their work that she was renting from us. He told me that her old boyfriend, who was deeply in love with her, also works together with them, and that she keeps her new place of residence a secret so that he would stop following her. He explained that the man was a drinker, and that when he drinks he becomes violent. She was scared that he would come here during a drinking episode. He said that her old boyfriend somehow found out that she was renting from us. I assured him that I have not told anyone about it, and even if he came I would call the police—there was nothing for her to be scared about. But as I said that to him, I was wondering what was really going on.

It seemed strange that she felt more comfortable talking to him about her needs related to the apartment, while it was obvious that she was avoiding talking to me, or even just looking into my eyes. But I explained that away for myself with the fact that it is more comfortable to talk to someone you have already worked with for two years. A restless feeling started to grow inside me, but I dismissed it. One day, he told me that he promised her I would take care of her cats. I was shocked that he would promise a tenant something that I would have to do, without even discussing it with me first.

It felt, as if he cared for this woman at my expense. I felt that his caring for her was much deeper than it should be with a tenant-landlord relationship. When I was about to express my disappointment, he explained that he could not say no to a best friend, and that she didn't have anybody to help her feed the two cats.

"What was I supposed to tell her?" he raised his voice, becoming defensive with me.

Then, he said that he also promised to her that I will change the cat litter box while she is away on long trips. I felt trapped: there was always trust between me and him, there was always support for each other when it was needed. I felt uneasy to say no to him, trying to be understanding about the fact that any friendship comes with obligations. Yet, I felt that something was not right about this whole situation. I began to feel very uncomfortable, trapped in the situation that I felt was forced onto me, a situation I did not know how to change without breaking the trust and connection between me and my husband.

5

Weeks went by. My husband and our tenant were often returning home together, which seemed suspiciously unusual to me, because all trips were scheduled differently. When they talked in the yard, he was smiling with a smile he has not given me for many years. She always returned home with a fresh, bright red lipstick on her lips. When our eyes met she would look down whenever she was passing me. She called him on the phone asking to come upstairs, using things that needed to be fixed in that apartment as an excuse to get him upstairs. It was obvious that they had a relationship growing between them. I decided to let him know how I felt about this. But talking about it only triggered a wave of irritation and defensiveness.

"I am trying to fix the apartment!" he yelled at me and added: "Do you want to do it yourself? Then do it! Why don't you go and fix it?"

There was logic in his words, as he was doing things or pretended to be doing things that I could not fix myself. He assured me that there was nothing going on between them, and that they were just friends. He said that he likes talking to her, and that he can not talk to me the way they talk to each other. I did not know what to say, as I felt that she could have come down to talk here to both of us if there was no intimacy involved. At the same time, I felt that they were closer than what he was able to admit to, and that even if she would have come downstairs, I would not feel comfortable having her here.

Noticing that things were going out of control, his co-workers started to call me, expressing their sympathy. I was told that Zachary and her have been scheduling their trips together for more than a year now, and that he was waiting for her after work each and every day, courting her. They told me that after work they went somewhere together in his car, then they came back to the parking lot and separated again. I noticed that he became more and more distant with me, until finally, I discovered that he leaves to work a few hours earlier than he is supposed to and comes back from work a few hours later than he is supposed to. I called him to ask what is going on. But he was very stern with me. I couldn't understand what it was that I did to him that changed him so much. What it was that drove him away from me so fast. Just a few months ago we had a conversation in which he stated that he would never leave me. Just a few months ago it seemed like we had a family. My heart felt discrepancy between what he told me and what he did. I kept asking him what was going on. He would become defensive and question me:

"Why are you asking? You had never asked me about this before."

One day, I opened his wallet in front of him, and he hurried to hide a hotel coupon to honeymoon suite so that I wouldn't be able to see it. He said that it was a present for me, and that he will give it to me someday, but for now he couldn't show me what it was. *Was it another hint that they were spending time at hotels while doing long trips together?* I wondered.

6

I decided to approach him again and do anything I could to return him back into the family. I told him that everyone at his job knows what is going on, and that I am willing to do anything to fix what is broken between us. But he denied everything his co-workers said about him and her. He kept saying that he can't talk to me about it right now, and that he would talk to me about it tomorrow. When "tomorrow" came, he would promise again to talk about it later. Weeks went by. He was returning home when I was already asleep, and leaving while I was still sleeping. The air felt so thick I could cut it with a knife. Finally, he came home when I was still awake, and I insisted we have a talk.

"I don't feel like talking about it right now," he said quickly. But realizing that he could not continue living in this lie, he came up to me and sat next to me on the bed. Looking at the wall with a dull, tired look, he said: "Whatever is broken between us, it is too late to fix."

We sat there for hours, talking about all the things we have been through together. He felt like he was empty inside. He did not have any feeling for me or the kids. He could not go on living with us. We were like a weight around his neck, pulling him down into the water. He felt like he was drowning, and this woman was like air for him. It was obvious that me and our kids became an obstacle to his happiness, and he could no longer be caged in the duality of his life.

He was living his new life for quite some time now and was ready for his freedom. He was ready to let go of everything that once had a deep meaning for him, everything that used to be so important to him. For me, on the other hand, it was a complete shock to find out that the man I lived with, the father of my children, was nothing more but a stranger whose heart and soul was given to another woman behind our back, in our own house. Crying, he started to confess that he can't live like this anymore, that he wanted us to sell the house and split the money in half. He wanted me to find another man and to be happy. He wanted me to keep our kids. He explained that our life together was good, but there were too many difficulties and responsibilities he didn't want to be part of any longer. He said, he came to this decision a while ago but couldn't bring himself to tell me about it. He told me that we had nothing in common anymore, nothing connected us, our children did not give him enough kisses, I didn't give him enough warmth, comfort, attention, a cozy home. He said that the only thing that would change with our separation will be us being able to see other people. This, of course, meant that it was him who needed to see other people. He assured me that even though we would get separated, nothing else will change between us. But as I found out later, it really meant that there would be no change for him to adjust to because he had nothing to lose. He had the person who loved him and who he loved dearly. The person who was able to give him escape from the life he did not want any longer. We were discarded. He concluded that he can't sleep with me in the same bed or be in a different room on the same floor any longer. So he packed his clothes, took his dresser, and moved upstairs in the room that was next to his "best friend."

7

I stood there in disbelief, watching him move. I felt like I was electrocuted. For him it was a relief to finally become free, to be closer to a person he loved more than anything else, more than his kids, me, or what used to be his family that was always there for him. For me it was so sudden, so hurtful, so unexpected, the fact that I lost him a long time ago, that I have lived in hope that things would improve, thinking that he is just too tired from work, that another weekend will come, and he will have it off to spend time together with us. I could not believe that he was having an affair in our own house, under the same roof, in front of our kids. I felt that I was treated disrespectfully, I felt humiliated. I felt powerless due to the fact that I was also a landlord to the woman who stole my husband. Therefore, I couldn't just come up and ask her to get out of my house.

Instead of accepting the loss, the next day I invited him for a walk in the park as if we still were a family. I told him that our kids would love to spend time with both of us. In the car he told kids about the situation. The children begged him not to leave the family. He told them that it was Mom who wanted the divorce, that he just wanted a separation, but Mom wanted all or nothing. He coldly told them that he would come to visit them, and that they should think of him as if he is gone to a long trip at work. By the time we reached the park, it was obvious that nothing I would do could change his mind. We didn't even get out of the car. We went back home, and he headed straight to his new room upstairs.

Grief and anxiety had paralyzed me. My mind was racing. I couldn't close my eyes all night, sitting in the rocking chair outside on the porch. I looked at the stars, shining in the dark sky above me, and I cried all the way to the morning. I met the sunrise together with singing birds, still wide awake. Watching the light filling the yard, I got up and with my bare feet went down the steps into the wet green grass. My mind just wouldn't calm down. I went back in the house, but hurtful feelings of grief and sorrow filled my heart. The house seemed too small for the feelings I had inside me, and I went outside on the porch again with tears streaming down my cheeks. Shaking silently, I swallowed the lump in my throat, weeping on the stairs of my big house that used to be my shelter from all problems and now transformed into the heart of hell. I couldn't believe the way we had to part after all we have been through together. I couldn't believe how cruelly I was treated by the person who I thought was part of me, was largest part of my life, my past, present, and future, my best friend, a father of my kids, a man I shared my life with for thirteen years. My thoughts were interrupted by the door slamming. My husband, in his white shirt and black pants, handsome and full of life, came out onto the porch demanding that I go inside. He told me that I was embarrassing him in front of our tenant. I was even hurt by his reaction to my pain and sorrow. I gathered all the strength that was left inside me, and looking in his shameless eyes, I told him that this was still my house, and no one would tell me where I should or shouldn't cry. Disappointed, he backed off into the house.

8

We went to file for divorce. The torture of being in the same house was unbearable. Every night he locked the door between our floors, while he was leaving both doors open during the day. It was obvious that the man I still loved had no respect for me. When our kids would come to visit him in the evening, he would rush them to the first floor saying that they needed to go to their mother. The kids would ask me why their father locks the door, telling me that they had to knock very hard to make him open the door for them. When he was passing through the first floor to get to his room upstairs, he was yelling at the kids for being loud, telling them that they disturb the tenant. Zachary had never said this to our children when the previous tenant was renting from us for at least eight years. The children could be themselves, and did not have to suppress their emotions at home, before his girlfriend moved in.

He was affectionate and caring with her, while he was icy cold with me, as if I was a complete stranger to him, as if we were never related. I meant nothing to him and had no value as a person. Apparently they started planning their future together a while ago. The property division conversations arose. He wanted to give her second floor of the same house. The idea of him being so cruel just couldn't fit into my mind. I explained that if she doesn't move out, I would have to evict her.

"You don't need the second floor," he commented coldly, "just give it to her, you and the kids will have enough."

He wasn't worried about how we would make ends meet. Her well being was the only thing on his mind, as if he was bewitched by her. He continued to deny that there was anything intimate between them. He kept convincing me that he couldn't live with me any longer but it didn't mean that he slept with her.

One day he came home earlier and went straight to shave and clean his teeth. In a few seconds he announced that he was tired and was heading to his room upstairs to sleep. He never used to go to sleep before midnight. I asked if he could stay with the kids—they missed him, and I could also use a breather. Very disappointed, he finally agreed to stay with the children. I went for a walk and came back home an hour later, the children were asleep in their beds way before their bed time. No one was supervising them on our floor. He was not home. I came up to his room upstairs—it was empty. As I was standing in the hallway between his and her rooms, her door opened, and he came out from her apartment. He, who was so shy about his ugly scar, was wearing nothing but his underwear. I made an attempt to open her door to talk to her, but he started restricting my movements, saying that if there is someone to blame it would only be him. He kept repeating that there was nothing between them, and that they just like talking to each other. I felt like I was sick to my stomach.

9

Three very long, painful months passed before they finally moved out. I couldn't take their affair in my house, it was damaging to me to be exposed to this cruelty. I asked him to move out, but he said that he couldn't do it because he needed money to pay for his new apartment. I gave him the money, and he found himself a place. Till the very last moment he lied to me that he was moving there alone. I was standing by the window, watching him lovingly help his new soul mate move her belongings. I caught her daughter's smiling eyes that were filled with apparent interest at my reaction on everything that was going on. His mistress got what she wanted; she had no feelings of shame or guilt. She was smiling also. She was amused. It was her victory.

He had the nerve to ask me for a key to my minivan, which he wanted to use to move her stuff. I refused to give it to him. When I showed some resistance to his cruelty, he got very upset. In the process of moving, he commented to our son to go to his room because he needed to talk to me, flavoring this torture with more insults and threats. He kept saying that this is still his house, and these are still his children, and that he has a right to come here as he pleases. He refused to give me the keys to the house. I found the strength to tell him that his home was no longer here, and that I would change the locks as soon as he leaves.

Watching them moving out together, feeling how empty my big house became, feeling the permanent irreversible loss, I could not go to sleep. My body was filled with adrenalin, and my mind was going through a severe anxiety attack. I didn't feel comfortable standing, sitting, or lying down. I couldn't find a place for myself; I could not find peace. It felt that I even lost myself somewhere in the middle of this emotional mess. It felt as if my heart would burst from the pain into small pieces. I had two children to care for, but I felt emotionally paralyzed. All this happened before we even got divorced. There I was, with not enough income to support my children and myself, I had no control over his child support payments as we were not divorced yet, and I had no more rental income. But I had a mortgage I needed to pay along with other important bills that could not wait. I begged him to convince her to return the keys to the apartment. But Zachary said that she had paid a month in advance and had a right to stay there until she felt she was ready to move out completely. So I could not rent the apartment out to anybody else.

10

It took me a long night of talking and assessing the situation with my friend, whose kindness and compassion was so deeply appreciated by me that night. I was facing a new turn of life once again. My mind was racing. My body had shakes. I was panicking. I needed money to sustain us. I made up a list of things I could sell and started moving towards my first goal—surviving alone with two children on my hands. My temporary goal was accomplished, as I sold a few things. One of them was a big air conditioner that previous tenants left behind. The night I sold it, Zachary came over to get it for his new family. When I explained to him that I sold it to make ends meet, he attacked me with yet another threat:

"I will show you money. I know what I will do to you." Then he stopped and said that he wouldn't even disclose his plans on how to punish me for selling something they so needed.

As summer went by, I reached my other goal—installed new windows in our kitchen which were bought together before he was stolen from me. I knew it would help me to keep our oil bills down. I installed it without his help, as this was his way of punishing me—he made himself unavailable when I needed help. Our old windows were so drafty that I was not scared of anything anymore. It could not be any worse. So I picked up a hammer and some screws, took the old windows out and put new ones in. My work did not look very pretty from the inside, but it was functioning properly and the house became much warmer. It was so rewarding to feel that I could still go on with my life without him. As I was ripping out the old window, I was relieving the anger that was pent up inside me.

11

Before I knew it, winter was at our door. I was glad that our house would be a little warmer, and our heating bills would be more affordable. Christmas time was just around the corner. I felt emotionally weak and knew that I couldn't make this time of year special for my children. My co-workers expressed their concerns that I stopped smiling and didn't socialize with them. They assured me that it's a time of year when miracles are bound to happen.

It was the day before Christmas when I walked into the office after a long day of work, tired and gloomy. There was a big basket with goodies on the table. It had a sign that read: "Tickets are $20 each." It was sitting there for a couple of months now. I did not have money to play, although the sign said that it would benefit a co-worker in need. In the middle of the office there were nicely wrapped boxes with pretty colorful bows on their tops. One by one, my co-workers were entering the room and adding more presents to the pile. I stood there observing it, feeling disappointed that I couldn't contribute to it this year. My co-workers walked around me with big smiles on their faces. *I wish I could put a smile like that on my face,* I thought to myself. *I could really use a smile to light up the holiday for my kids,* I admitted to myself sadly.

"We did this for you and your kids," said the voice behind my back with a shade of joy. "You see that basket there? We collected some money for you," my manager added.

I stood there, overwhelmed with joy. I looked at the pile of presents again, trying to make a connection between my broken life and this act of kindness. I almost felt like my body went floating in the air, as I felt so touched.

"For me? For me and my kids?" I stood there in disbelief, taken by surprise, feeling the presence of the goose bumps on my skin.

As I stood there, completely overwhelmed, they were putting money and presents into my hands. Sobbing like a lost child, I was giving them big, lasting hugs in return. They helped me to carry the presents to my minivan. As I was driving home, I couldn't see anything in the mirror. My van was packed from the floor all the way up to the top. I got home and my heart felt so big that I had to express my feelings on paper. I returned to work with a card where I wrote:

> To my coworkers—Santas:
>
> I have never felt so much love.
> I have never seen hearts this big.
> When I thought we were all alone
> We got presents and money to live…
>
> There's no words to express how I feel.
> I have never felt like this, ever.
> I will carry your kindness with me.
> It will stay in my heart forever!

I brought the boxes and bags into my house and spread them out on the floor near the Christmas tree. They took up the whole room. I locked the door to that room wondering what my kids reaction would be when they discovered such an abundance of presents. My children had never gotten so many presents before in their lives. That evening, before we went to sleep, I said a prayer to God, thanking him for the miracles in my life. I put the kids to sleep and unlocked the door to the room filled with gifts.

12

As time went by, I realized that my emotional stability and peace in my heart was the key to my children's happiness. I discovered that by allowing Zachary to speak to me on the phone, threatening me, insulting me, and letting him in the house, I only set myself up for falling apart again. I needed to get stronger. It seemed like he derived pleasure from threatening me and hurting me. It was obvious that they both paired up against me, that he followed her advice on how to get out the most of this separation. Our powers were not equal. He had a supportive person next to him, who made him feel like a man, who gave him a gentle touch he needed, who was listening to him attentively. I had no one by my side, no one to be close with, no one to give me the emotional and financial support he could get from her. I decided that I should not let him hurt me anymore. I should make every effort to take away every chance he gets to control and run my life. I told him that we would communicate through email, and that I will no longer answer his phone calls. I explained that if there is a problem with this, then he should feel free to ask court for a mediator who will relate our messages to each other. His voice and his body was like a voice and body of the person I loved, but his heart was a heart of a stranger, the enemy. It felt like there was a snake inside him that was ready to attack me to death at any given moment. Now that he and his girlfriend were out of my house, I isolated myself from him and her, disabling their plan to hurt me more.

13

We got our divorce. I was hoping that I will never see that woman again. But I was wrong. Their cruelty had no limits. On days when he picked up our kids for visitations he would bring her along. It was painful enough to see the man I still had feelings for with the woman, but she had a nerve to come to my yard after breaking up the family the way she did. I asked him to not bring her here anymore. His response to my request was:

"Why not? We are divorced, I can do whatever I want now."

Feeling that I have had enough of cruelty and humiliation, I went straight to the sheriff's office and filed a no trespassing order for this heartless woman—the best friend of an insensitive man. As she was served with a no trespassing order, he called me and left an angry message that he doesn't understand why I had to be so cruel to her. He was sending me on a guilt trip! In a few months, I found out they bought a house together. Aside from the thought that this was planned long before he even talked to me about divorce, it was very painful to know that my children will be spending time at her house during the visitations.

A year filled with pain and grief went by. I could not find anybody to replace the person I loved. I knew that person did not exist anymore, that it was the same body and same voice, but the person was long gone. Other men did not feel right, thoughtful enough, caring enough, respectful enough. My body was hungry for a gentle touch. The touch no one could give because it was the touch of the loving person my body was missing, the touch of a person who I loved in return. I was surviving, I had a roof over my head and the kids were with me, but I couldn't stop grieving the loss of the person I loved and devoted myself completely to, the loss of the person who loved me and cared for me the way he cared for that woman. I was having a hard time recovering from the cruelty I was treated with. Depression set in so deep that nothing mattered anymore.

One of my friends, who I cheered up years ago inspiring her to go to church, invited me to join her there. She reminded me about my own words that God will send us people and will take them away from us, but He will always be there for us, with us. She took me to her church. Their songs deeply touched my heart. I was standing in the aisle, whispering the words of the song that were projected onto the wall in front of me, while the live music filled all the corners of my broken heart:

> "When the oceans rise and thunders roar
> I will soar with you above the storm
> Father You are King over the flood
> I will be still and know you are God."*

These lines had such a deep meaning to me. There were so many things time could not erase from my heart. There were so many miracles bound together with sorrows and pain. I covered my face with my hands and, shaking silently, I wept. The memories about times that I spent with Zachary at the hospital trauma intensive care came up again. Those were memories when I prayed that God would take my life instead and breathe it into his broken body. I felt the loss of peace, self, family, loved one, loss of support, feeling of loneliness, all these feelings were choking me right here, right now. A young woman came up and sat next to me. She put tissues on my lap and started praying for me aloud. Squeezing my hand, she whispered in my ear: "May God guide you onto the right path. Dear God, please help her, please comfort her."

Shaking like a leaf in the wind, I wept, swallowing the lump in my throat. I felt that God was there with me, I felt his presence and loving care in the squeeze of a stranger's hand; I felt home. The song changed into a different one, and I eventually calmed down. We exchanged our names. She looked at me with her beautiful brown eyes that were shining with a light of compassion, as if silently asking "What happened?" My heart felt overwhelmed. She asked:

"Is there anything I can do for you?"

I looked in her beautiful sincere eyes, squeezed her hand one more time before saying "Thank you" and left the church. As I got home, I sat in the rocking chair outside my big empty house, enjoying warm summer breeze. I opened my bible, and two dried rose petals flew into the air, being caught with a gust of wind.

* "Still" © 2002 Reuben Morgan/Hillsong Publishing

Printed in the United States
154347LV00010B/35/P

9 781604 417869